My name is Sinque Morrison, the author of the books, San Bernardino Man, Parts 1, 2 and 3. One of the reasons that I wrote these books was to assist young people in determining how to resolve anger issues that they may have, in a nonviolent way.

Unfortunately, when I was growing-up I was bullied incessantly, and as a result of this, I tried to resolve the issues with my oppressors in a negative way and suffered the consequences of this.

Now, I am able to use comprehensive alternatives to resolve contentious situations in a more harmonious manner.

One of these positive measures, is to take a deep breath and walk away from any toxic situations.

As a consequence of this, I have become empowered in handling acrimonious situations in a calm fashion. Thereby, taking into consideration, the care, as well as respect, for all involved.

My prayer, is that all those who are reading this book, will develop the necessary skills in addressing hostile
environments, that they may find themselves in, in a strife free manner.

Anthony's father had passed away from the brutal assault by Bad Nefarious.

Anthony's mother explained to him that his father's dying wish was that Anthony would do something valuable with his life. She went on to tell Anthony that his father had left something of excellent value for him at his uncle Baszine's house.

Anthony visited his uncle Baszine.

He discovered that his father had left him a map which would lead him to a powerful magical potion.

Anthony followed the map to the cemetery on the west side of the city. As he approached the gravestone that was marked on the map; a large, glass coffin with a grotesque, cross-eyed bottled green leprechaun arose on top of it; and handed him the magic potion.

The leprechaun had a wide-opened mouth with large, razor sharped fangs that glistened in the sunlight.

Beneath the leprechaun, inside of the large glass coffin, was a terrifying monster with gross, pointed fangs. It was roaring and bellowing a strange, unknown language.

Anthony stood back in shock, wondering what would happen next!

The leprechaun notified Anthony, in a low, quaking voice not to use the magic potion until he had learnt how to control his temper. The leprechaun also warned Anthony that once the potion was used, there was no turning back.

CEMETERY

On the other side of San Bernardino, the police thought they had cornered Bad Nefarious in a dark, street alley.

Unfortunately, Bad Nefarious was too smart for the cops, he managed to escape them by soaring high above them with his large, green, curved shaped wings.

As he flew higher, he breathed out grey, ashy smoke from his broad, outstretched mouth.

The police were perplexed! They were at a loss for what to do next.

BN
P OLIC

The public ran in fear and panic as they saw what was going on, Bad Nefarious enjoyed the pandemonium, he terrorized the public further by flying over them, pumping out vast, far-reaching flames of fire, simultaneously, landing his tremendous feet indiscriminately on the heads of the terrified public.

BN

The public, as well as the police were petrified, but Bad Nefarious was merciless, totally unrelenting.

He tormented all members of the public, no-one was safe!

The worst was yet to come... not content with his own personal reign of terror, Bad Nefarious commanded all the inhumane, hideous, vicious, monsters and aliens from the spaceship to join him in his brutal onslaught on the people of San Bernardino, California.

Every type of abhorrent, untamed alien departed from the spaceship to join Bad Nefarious in his carnage against the people.

Many humans were forced to bow down in humiliation to the aliens or face torture.

STOP

Out of immense fear, members of the public started turning on each other, as they felt they had no-one to protect them.

There was not one single person courageous enough to stop Bad Nefarious or his aliens from the warfare that they were inflicting on the town.

No-one was safe from the attackers from out of space!

Petrified children fled into the seemingly, safe, quiet subway; under the false belief that Bad Nefarious would not be able to discover them there.

Nevertheless, Bad Nefarious came upon them – and when he did, he was able to control them by putting deep, hypnotic spells on each of them – so that they would obey his every command.

BN

A beautiful family from London, England that had recently moved to San Bernardino, were not spared from Bad Nefarious's ruthless attacks.

He flew over Krisanne and her family tormenting them with his hot, fiery, suffocating smoke.

"What a welcome to the city!"

Cried out Krisanne as she and her loved ones ran for safety under the Red Rock Bridge.

Jordan
''Jerome
Krisanne
Jayden
Jana

Anthony was fed up! He knew that he couldn't just stand by and watch the people from his hometown being tortured and abused.

He knew what he had to do, he sipped, swigged, then drank the magic potion…but the bottle accidentally, slipped out of Anthony's hands, it hit the floor! A stray dog lapped up the rest of it.

As the potion took effect, Anthony felt a strange, warm fuzzy feeling in his whole body, it started off as a little tingle, then an awkward sensation.

He started to dance wildly, shaking and moving violently.

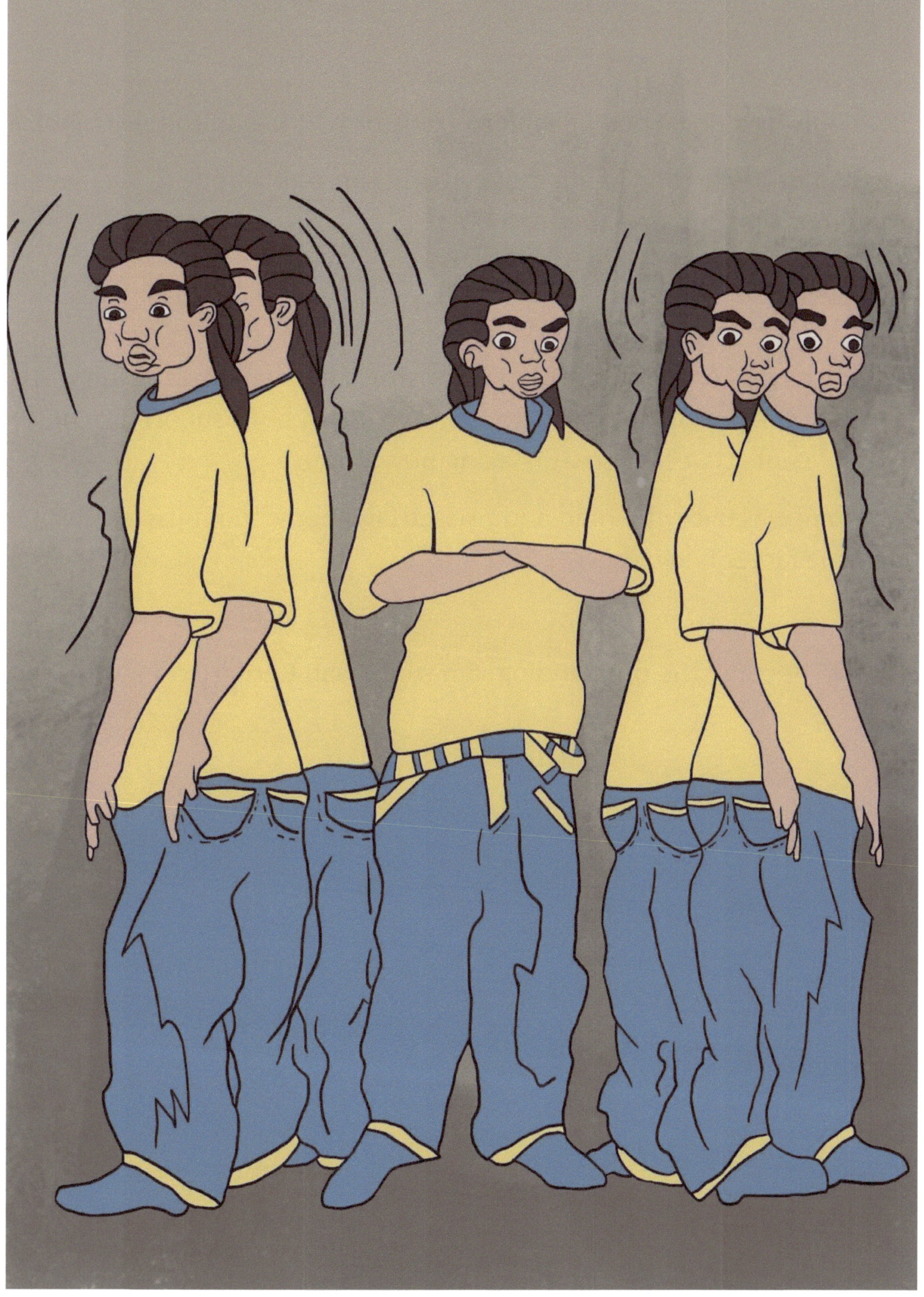

Suddenly, the dog's body began to transform, it began to twist vigorously.

Instead of having one head, it developed three! It's body metamorphosised into that of a horse.

Anthony, later named it 'Ghetto Dog', it was a hybrid, a dog with three heads and the body of a horse.

Astonishingly, Anthony started to transform himself! As a result of drinking the potion, his body transmuted into a buff, superhuman, magnificent, majestic, breath-taking powerhouse.

Anthony was overwhelmed and excited! His body and muscles became larger and larger!

He had become the outstanding, amazing, 'San Bernardino Man.'

HEY KIDS, IF YOU SEE SOMEONE BEING BULLIED TELL AN ADULT OR SOMEONE THAT YOU CAN TRUST. BEING BULLIED IS A TERRIBLE THING, IT CAN CAUSE STRESS, AS WELL AS DEPRESSION. SOMETIMES, IT CAN LEAD TO SUICIDE.
REMEMBER, BULLIES ARE COWARDS SO WE ALL MUST FIND A WAY TO STAND UP TO THEM.

LIFE IS ABOUT LOVE AND PEACE. STAY STRONG AND KEEP LOVE IN YOUR HEART.

"ONE LOVE FROM SINQUE"

COMING SOON:
SAN BERNARDINO MAN PART 3

<u>Dedication</u>

This dedication is to all young victims of violent crimes, as well as to the many women and men who have suffered from the devastating crime of domestic violence.

Remember, that there are many people and organisations that you can talk to about any violent crimes that you may have been a victim of.

I would also like to dedicate this book to the teenagers and young adults who have joined gangs due to peer pressure, or because they have been coerced or bullied into doing so.

If you would like to talk to me about any of the issues mentioned in this book, you can contact me on:

SINQUEMORRISON@Getting out.com .

I would also like to dedicate this book to my children, Anthony, Cereniti, Quenique, Clarence and Alexis; and to my stepchildren, Jayden, Jerome, Jana, and Jordan.

I also dedicate this book to my grandchildren, and to my own very special lady, my precious mother, Diane.

I would also like to say a very special thankyou to the most beautiful woman in my life, Krisanne Simmons-Smith, for over four years now, we have been together. If it wasn't for your love and patience, this book would have never been published.

You have worked extremely hard to have the book published so quickly, and I appreciate everything that you have done for me.

I love you, more than I have loved anyone, you are a very smart and beautiful person, on the inside and out.

I would also like to dedicate this book to my late father, Clyde Edwards. I love and miss you pops, rest in peace.

I would also like to thank my brother, Baybra-Rocc, for helping to fund the publishing of this book.

And finally, I would like to say thankyou to my amazing step-son, Jayden Smith, who spent days and nights helping to publish the book.

He also helped with the graphics and design of the pictures.

Jayden, I am so grateful to you, because you helped to fund the costs of publishing the book from your own pocket. Jayden, you have a good heart and a God-given talent for computers, art, design and graphics.

Thankyou so much for your help and support, I love and appreciate you.

Sinque Morrison